Arabian Nights

Retold from the original
by Martin Woodside

Illustrated by Lucy Corvino

STERLING CHILDREN'S BOOKS
New York

STERLING CHILDREN'S BOOKS
New York

An Imprint of Sterling Publishing
387 Park Avenue South
New York, NY 10016

STERLING CHILDREN'S BOOKS and the distinctive Sterling Children's Books logo are trademarks of Sterling Publishing Co., Inc.

ISBN 978-1-4027-4573-7

Library of Congress Cataloging-in-Publication Data

Woodside, Martin.
  Arabian nights : retold from the original / abridged by Martin Woodside ; illustrated by Lucy Corvino.
    p. cm.—(Classic starts)
  Summary: An abridged version of the tale of Scheherazade, daughter of King Shahryar's advisor, who tells her husband, the king, a different story every night to keep him from fulfilling his plan to kill her in the morning.
  ISBN-13: 978-1-4027-4573-7
  ISBN-10: 1-4027-4573-7
  [1. Fairy tales. 2. Folklore—Arab countries. 3. Arabs—Folklore.] I. Corvino, Lucy, ill. II. Title.

PZ8.W867Arb 2008
[398.2]—dc22

2007015205

Distributed in Canada by Sterling Publishing
$^c/o$ Canadian Manda Group, 165 Dufferin Street,
Toronto, Ontario, Canada M6K 3H6
Distributed in the United Kingdom by GMC Distribution Services,
Castle Place, 166 High Street, Lewes, East Sussex, England BN7 1XU
Distributed in Australia by Capricorn Link (Australia) Pty. Ltd.
P.O. Box 704, Windsor, NSW 2756, Australia

For information about custom editions, special sales, and premium and corporate purchases, please contact Sterling Special Sales at 800-805-5489 or specialsales@sterlingpublishing.com.

Printed in China

Lot#:
6 8 10 9 7
07/13

www.sterlingpublishing.com/kids

CONTENTS

The Story of King Shahryar and Scheherazade

It is said that long ago there lived two great kings, brothers named Shahryar and Shahzaman. Shahryar was older, and his power reached the farthest parts of the earth.

Shahryar felt a desire to see his brother and asked his vizier, who was the king's chief minister, to go bring his brother to him. When Shahzaman arrived, his brother hugged him. The two brothers spent the whole day at each other's side, and Shahryar couldn't help notice that his brother looked pale and ill.

The days passed, and Shahzaman continued wasting away. Shahryar thought his brother was homesick, but it turned out to be something much worse. After ten days, Shahzaman broke down and told his brother what lay at the root of his sorrows. His wife, the queen, had left him, and he was heartbroken. He told Shahryar the story of how he had been betrayed, and the great king could not believe his ears.

After hearing his brother's tale, Shahryar became enraged, so enraged that he lost his senses. He decided that no woman could ever be trusted and planned something terrible. The king summoned his vizier and told him to find him a wife. He intended to wed her for a single day and then kill her. He would continue to do this until all the women in his kingdom were gone.

Now, the vizier had an older daughter called Scheherazade and a younger one called Dinarzad. The older daughter had read many books and was

well educated. When she heard of the king's evil plan, she said to her father, "I would like you to marry me to King Shahryar, so that I may either save our people or die like all the rest."

When the vizier heard what his daughter said, he was very angry and forbid her to marry the king. The two argued for a long time, but Scheherazade would not change her mind. So he sent his daughter to be to the king, saying, "May God not take you from me."

Scheherazade was very happy and, after preparing herself and packing what she needed, went to her younger sister Dinarzad. "Sister," she said, "listen well to me. When I go to the king, I will send for you, and when you come say, 'Sister, if you are not sleepy, tell a story.' This will cause the king to let me go and will save the people of the kingdom. You must trust this plan."

Dinarzad replied, "Very well."

That night, the vizier took Scheherazade to the great King Shahryar, and she was wed to him. But when Shahryar went to bed that night, Scheherazade wept. The king asked her why she was crying, and she replied, "I have a sister, and I wish to bid her good-bye."

Then the king sent for the sister, who arrived and sat at the foot of the bed. Dinarzad said, "Sister, if you are not sleepy, tell us one of your lovely little tales to pass the night, for I am afraid to be without you."

Scheherazade turned to King Shahryar and said, "May I have permission to tell a story?" He replied, "Yes," and Scheherazade was very happy. "Listen," she said.

CHAPTER 1

The Tale of the Merchant and His Wife

༄

THE FIRST NIGHT

It is said, O wise and happy King, that there once was a rich merchant who planned a visit to another country. He filled his bags with bread and dates and mounted his horse. For many nights, he traveled under God's care until he reached his destination. When his visit was finished, he turned for home. He traveled for three days, and on the fourth day he found an orchard and went in to shade himself from the sun. He sat by a stream under a walnut tree, pulled out some loaves of bread and a handful of dates, and began to eat, throwing the date pits right and left until he'd had enough. Then he got up and said his prayers.

He had hardly finished when he saw an old demon before him with a sword in his hand, standing with his feet on the ground and his head in the clouds. The demon screamed, "Get up, so that I may kill you with this sword, just as you have killed my son."

The merchant was scared. He said, "By God, I did not kill your son. How could that have been?" The demon said, "Didn't you sit down, take out some dates from your bag, and eat, throwing the pits about you?" The merchant replied, "Yes, I did." The demon said, "As you were throwing the pits, my son happened to be walking by and was struck and killed by one of them, and I must now kill you."

The merchant said, "O my lord, please don't kill me." The demon replied, "By God, I must kill you, as you killed my son." The merchant said, "If I killed him, I did it by mistake. Please forgive me." The demon replied, "I must kill you," and he seized the merchant and threw him to the ground.

The merchant began to weep for his wife and children. The demon raised his sword while the merchant was drenched in tears, saying, "There is no power or strength, save in God the Mighty."

But morning drew near at this point in the story, and Scheherazade fell silent, leaving King Shahryar burning to hear the rest of the tale. Then Dinarzad said to her sister, "What a strange and lovely story!" Scheherazade replied, "This is nothing compared with what I will tell you tomorrow night, if the king spares me and lets me live. It will be even better and more entertaining." The king thought, "I will spare her until I hear the rest of the story. Then I will have her put to death the next day."

THE SECOND NIGHT

King Shahryar worked all the next day and returned home at night to Scheherazade. Then Dinarzad said to her sister, "Please, sister, if you are not sleepy, tell us one of your lovely little stories." The king added, "Let it be the end of the story of the demon and the merchant." Scheherazade replied, "With the greatest pleasure, dear, happy King."

It is said, O wise and happy King, that when the demon raised his sword, the merchant begged the demon, "Please let me say good-bye to my family, and my wife and children, before you kill me." The demon asked, "Do you swear to God that if I let you go, you will come back one year from this day?" The merchant replied, "Yes, I swear to God."

After the merchant swore this, the demon let him go, and he mounted his horse and went on his way. He finally reached his home and came to his wife and children. When he saw them, he wept bitterly. His wife asked him, "Husband, what is the matter with you? Why are you sad when we are happy, celebrating your return?" He replied, "Why not be sad when I have only one year to live?" Then he told her everything that had happened with the demon.

When his family heard what he said, they began to cry. It was a day of sadness as all the children gathered around their father. The merchant spent the rest of the year this way. Then he said his prayers and bid his family good-bye. His sons hung around his neck, his daughters wept, and his wife wailed. He said to them, "Children, this is God's will." He turned away, got on his horse, and traveled until he reached the orchard.

He sat at the place where he had eaten the dates, waiting with tearful eyes for the demon. As he waited, an old man, leading two dogs on a leash, approached and greeted him, and he returned the greeting. The old man asked,

"Friend, why do you sit here in this place full of demons and devils? For in this haunted orchard, there is only sorrow."

The merchant told him everything that had happened with the demon. The old man was amazed at the tale and said, "Your promise to return here is a brave one. By God, I will not leave you until I see what happens with the demon." Then he sat down beside him and they chatted.

But morning drew near Scheherazade, and she fell silent. As the day dawned, Dinarzad said to her sister, "What a strange and lovely story!" Scheherazade replied, "Tomorrow night, I will tell you something even better and more entertaining."

THE THIRD NIGHT

The next night, Dinarzad said to her sister, "Please, sister, if you are not sleepy, tell us one of your lovely little stories." The king added, "Let it be the end of the merchant's story, for I would like to hear it." Scheherazade replied, "As you wish."

I heard, O happy King, that as the merchant and the man with the two black dogs sat talking, they suddenly saw the dust rise, and when it cleared they saw the demon approaching with a steel sword in his hand. He stood before them without greeting and said to the merchant, "Get ready to die." The merchant and the old man began to weep.

The old man with the black dogs approached the demon, and said, "If I tell you what happened to me and to these two dogs, and if you find it stranger and more amazing than what happened to you and the merchant, will you set him free?" The demon replied, "I will."

So the old man began to tell his story:

Demon, these two dogs are my brothers. When our father died, he left behind three sons and gave us each an equal sum of money. Each of us took our money and became a shopkeeper. Soon my older brother, one of these dogs, sold the contents of his shop and left on a trip to trade goods overseas for a lot of money. A full year went by, when I saw one day a beggar in my shop.

"Don't you recognize me?" the beggar asked tearfully, and when I looked at him closely, I saw that it was my older brother. I hugged him and took him into the shop, asking him what had happened to him. He replied, "My money is gone."

I took him home with me and gave him half the money I had. I said, "Live your life as if you had never been this way." He gladly took the money and opened another shop.

Soon afterward, my second brother, this other dog, decided to take a trading trip as well. We tried to stop him, but he would not listen. A year later, he came back just like his brother. I said to him, "Brother, didn't I tell you not to go?" He cried and said, "Brother, I have lost everything."

I took him home with me. After we had something to eat, I told him that I would divide my money equally with him. He opened another shop, and the three of us stayed together for a while. Eventually, my two brothers asked me to go on a trading trip with them, but I said no, asking, "Did you learn nothing from your adventures?"

They dropped the matter, and for six years we worked in our stores, buying and selling, but every year they asked me to go on a trading trip with them. Finally, I said, "Brothers, I am ready to go with you. How much money do you have?"

They had wasted all their money, but my shop had grown. So I divided my money into two parts. I split one part among the three of us and said, "I will bury the other half in the ground, in case what happened to you happens to me." They replied, "This is an excellent idea."

After I closed my shop, we bought trading goods, rented a large ship, and set off, sailing all day and night for a month.

But morning drew near Scheherazade, and she fell silent. As the day dawned, Dinarzad said to her sister, "What a strange and lovely story!" Scheherazade replied, "Tomorrow night, I will tell you something even stranger, if our great God lets me live another day."

THE FOURTH NIGHT

The next night, Dinarzad said to her sister, "Please, sister, if you are not sleepy, tell us one of your lovely little stories." The king added, "Let it be the end of the merchant's story, for I would like to hear it." Scheherazade replied, "With great pleasure."

I heard, O happy King, that the old man continued telling his story to the demon:

For a month, my brothers and I sailed the salty sea until we came to a port city. We entered the city and sold our goods, buying other goods to take back to the ship. When we got to the seashore, I met a woman who was dressed in rags. She kissed my hands and said, "O my lord, do me a favor, and I believe I will be able to reward you for it." I replied, "I will do you a favor without reward." She said, "O my lord, marry me and take me with you on this boat."

I felt pity for her and, guided by God, I agreed. I gave her a beautiful dress, and we were married. Then I took her to the boat, and we sailed off again. I felt great love for her and stayed with her day and night, ignoring my brothers.

Meanwhile, my brothers grew jealous of me and plotted to kill me. One night, they waited until I was asleep beside my wife. Then they carried the two of us and threw us into the sea.

When we awoke, my wife turned into a spirit and carried me across the sea to an island. In the morning, she said, "Husband, I have rewarded you by saving you from drowning. When I saw you by the seashore, I felt love for you and came to you in disguise, and you accepted my love. But now I must kill your brothers."

When I heard what she said, I was amazed, and I thanked her for saving me. I told her all that happened to us since our father had died, from beginning to end. When she heard my story, she was very angry and said, "I will fly to your brothers now and sink their boat."

"For God's sake, don't," I said. "They are my brothers, after all." Eventually, I managed to soothe her. She flew away with me, setting me on the roof of my house. I climbed down and dug up the money I had buried. Then I went out, greeting the people in the market, and reopened my shop.

When I came home that evening, I found these two dogs tied up. As soon as they saw me, they came to me and wept and rubbed themselves against me. I suddenly heard my wife say, "O my lord, these are your brothers. They will stay in this condition for ten years. Only after ten years will they be men again." Then she told me where to find her, and she left.

The ten years have passed, and I was on my way with my brothers to have my wife lift the spell when I met this man here. When I asked about his own story, he told me you were going to kill him, and I promised not to leave him until I found out what

happened between you. This is my story. Isn't it amazing?

The demon replied, "By God, as you promised, it is a strange and amazing story. You win. I will spare this man's life." Then the demon let the man go and departed. The merchant thanked the old man, and the old man congratulated him on his freedom. The merchant went back home to his family and lived with them for many years until the day he died.

But morning drew near Scheherazade, and she fell silent. Dinarzad said to her sister, "What a strange and lovely story!" Scheherazade replied, "Tomorrow night, I will tell you the story of the fisherman, which is even more amazing."

CHAPTER 2

The Story of the Fisherman and the Demon

⌒

THE FIFTH NIGHT

The next night, Dinarzad said to her sister, "Please, sister, if you are not sleepy, tell us one of your lovely little tales." The king said, "Let it be the story of the fisherman." Scheherazade replied, "As you wish."

It is said that there was a very old fisherman who had a wife and three daughters. They were so poor that they did not even have enough food to get them through each day. This fisherman cast his net four times a day.

One day, while the moon was still up and the morning was young, he went out with his net past the outskirts of the city to the seashore. Then he waded out into the water, cast his net, and waited for it to sink. He gathered the rope and started to pull, feeling it get heavier and heavier, until he was unable to pull it any farther. He took off his clothes and dove into the water, swimming under the net and shaking and pulling at it until he finally brought it to shore.

Feeling quite happy, he went to open the net. But when he did, he found only a large, empty jar. The fisherman felt sad after all his work and said, "This is a strange catch!"

The fisherman prayed, cleaned his net, mended it, and set it out to dry. Then he waded back into the water and cast his net again. Once again the net got stuck, and once again the fisherman had to dive into the water to free it. When he pulled the net to shore and looked inside, tears filled his eyes. There was nothing in the net but a rotten old log. "This is the strangest day!" he cried.

The fisherman again laid his net out to dry, and again prayed to God. When the net was dry, he cast it a third time and waited for it to sink. This time when he pulled the net up, he found nothing inside but broken bottles and stones. He wept at his bad luck.

Then the fisherman raised his eyes to the heavens and said, "O Lord, you know that I cast my net only four times each day. I have already cast it three times, and there is only one more try left. Lord, let the sea help me!"

He cast his net into the water a fourth time and watched it sink. When he pulled, the net didn't move. He shook it and found that it was caught at the bottom. Once again, he dove into the water, and he worked a long time to shake the net free and drag it to shore. There was something heavy inside. When he opened the net, he saw a large brass jar with a stopper at the end.

The fisherman was happy, saying to himself, "I will sell it at the market, for it must be worth a lot of money." He tried to move the jar, but it was so heavy that he was unable to budge it. He decided to remove the stopper and pour out the contents. Using his knife, he finally worked the stopper loose. Then he tilted the jar to the ground and shook it, but nothing came out. He was very surprised.

After a while, though, a great cloud of smoke rose, getting bigger and bigger until it hid the daylight. For a long time, the smoke kept rising from the jar. Then it gathered and took shape, and there stood a demon with his feet on the ground and his head in the clouds. He had a head like a fortress, a mouth like a cave, and great fangs for teeth.

When the fisherman saw him, he shook with terror, his jaw froze, and his mouth went dry.

But morning drew near Scheherazade, and she fell silent. Dinarzad said to her sister, "Sister, what an amazing story!" Scheherazade replied, "Tomorrow night I will tell you something even more amazing, if I stay alive."

THE SIXTH NIGHT

The following night, Dinarzad said, "Please, sister, tell us another one of your lovely stories." The king added, "Let it be the end of the story of the demon and the fisherman." Scheherazade replied, "With the greatest pleasure!"

I heard, O happy King, that the fisherman asked, "Demon, why are you in this jar?" The demon replied, "Be glad!" The fisherman asked "Glad of what?" The demon added, "Be glad that you will be soon put to death."

The fisherman frowned at this and said, "Why do you wish to kill me when I have brought you back into this world?"

The demon replied, "Make a wish!" The fisherman was happy again and said, "What will I wish for?" The demon replied, "Tell me how you wish to die."

The fisherman asked, "Is this my reward for having freed you from the jar?" The demon replied, "Fisherman, listen to my story. I angered God and he put me in this brass jar and sealed it tight. Then he threw me into the sea. I stayed there for two hundred years, thinking, 'Whoever sets me free, I will make him rich.' But the two hundred years went by and no one set me free. When I entered the next hundred years, I promised myself, 'Whoever saves me, I will make him king and grant him three wishes every day,' but that hundred years passed by, and more years still, and no one set me free. Then I raged and growled and said to myself, 'Whoever sets me free from now on, I will let him choose himself the manner of his death.' Soon you came by and set me free. So tell me how you wish to die."

When the fisherman heard what the demon said, he replied, "To God we belong and to him we return. After all these years, with all my bad luck, I had to set you free now. Spare me, and God will grant you his forgiveness. But destroy me, and God will destroy you." The demon replied again, "Tell me how you wish to die."

Now the fisherman was certain he was going to die. He wept, saying, "O my children, may we not be taken from each other." Again he turned to the demon and said, "For God's sake, let me go as a reward for setting you free from this jar." The demon replied, "Your death is your reward for saving me."

Then the fisherman thought to himself, "He is only a demon, while I am a human being. I am smarter than him." Then he asked, "Will you promise to answer one question before you kill me?" The demon said, "Ask."

But morning drew near Scheherazade, and she fell silent. Dinarzad said to her sister, "Sister, what a strange and amazing story!" Scheherazade replied, "This is nothing compared with what I will tell you tomorrow night."

THE SEVENTH NIGHT

The following night, Dinarzad said, "Please, sister, tell us another of your amazing little tales." The king added, "Let it be the end of the story of the demon and the fisherman." Scheherazade replied, "With the greatest pleasure!"

I heard, O King, that the fisherman said to the demon, "By God, tell me whether you were really inside this jar." The demon replied, "By God, I was a prisoner in this jar." The fisherman said, "You are lying. This jar is not even large enough for one of your hands. How can it be large enough to fit your whole body?" The demon replied, "Don't you believe that I was inside?" The fisherman said, "No, I don't."

So the demon shook himself and turned into smoke, which rose, stretched over the sea, spread over the land, then gathered and began to enter the jar. When the smoke disappeared, the demon shouted from within, "Fisherman, do you believe me now?"

The fisherman at once took the stopper and clamped it back onto the opening of the jar. Then he cried out, "Now, demon, tell me how *you* wish to die. For I will throw you into this sea, build a house right here on the shore, and warn any fisherman who comes along about the demon who will let him choose how he wishes to die."

The demon realized that the fisherman had tricked him. "Fisherman, don't do this to me," he said. "I was only joking with you."

The fisherman replied, "You are the dirtiest and meanest of all demons." Then he started to roll the jar toward the sea. The demon shouted, "Don't! Don't!" but the fisherman answered, "Yes! Yes!"

Finally, in a soft voice, the demon asked, "Fisherman, if you open the jar, I will make you rich." The fisherman replied, "You are lying, and I will punish you by throwing this jar to the bottom of the sea!"

The demon cried out, "Fisherman, don't do it! Set me free this time, and I pledge never to bother you or harm you but to make you rich." When he heard this, the fisherman made the demon promise to God that if the fisherman released him and let him out, he would not harm him but make him rich.

After the demon made this promise, the fisherman opened the jar, and the smoke began to rise again. When the demon emerged, he kicked the jar away, sending it flying into the middle of the sea. When he saw this, the fisherman was sure he would soon be dead. Still, he cried out, "Demon, you made a promise to God. Do not betray me, or God will destroy you."

The demon laughed when he heard what the fisherman said. He replied, "Fisherman, follow me," and the fisherman followed him until they came to a mountain outside the city. They climbed over to the other side of the mountain and came to a forest. In the middle of the forest stood a lake surrounded by four hills.

The fisherman looked at the lake with wonder, for it was full of fish of many colors. The demon told the fisherman to cast his net. He did so, then pulled back the net along with four fish: one white, one red, one blue, and one yellow.

The demon said to him, "Now take them to the king of your city, and he will give you enough to make you rich. But don't fish here more than once a day." Then the demon kicked the ground, and it opened up and swallowed him whole.

The fisherman, O King, did as he was told, and he sold the fish for a good sum of money. Every day he went back to the mysterious lake and every day he caught four fish — one white, one red, one blue, and one yellow — and then sold them to the king. After this, his wife and children never went through the day without food. They were all quite happy, and the fisherman counted his blessings for the day he'd met the terrible demon.

But morning drew near Scheherazade, and she fell silent. Dinarzad said to her sister, "Sister, what a strange and amazing story!" Scheherazade replied, "This is nothing compared with the story I will tell you tomorrow, if I am still alive."

CHAPTER 3

The Porter's Tale

⌒

THE EIGHTH NIGHT

The following night, when Scheherazade was in bed, her sister Dinarzad said, "Please, sister, tell us another one of your lovely tales." The king added, "Let it be even more amazing than the story of the demon and the fisherman." Scheherazade replied, "With the greatest pleasure!"

I heard, O happy King, there once lived in the city of Baghdad a young man who worked as a porter, carrying goods and delivering them. One day he was standing in the market, leaning on his basket, when a woman came up to him. She wore a silk veil and a fine gold scarf. When she lifted her face, the young man saw that she had beautiful dark eyes. Then with a soft voice, she said "Porter, take your basket and follow me."

The porter took his basket and hurried behind her, saying, "O lucky day, O happy day." She walked in front of him until she came to a house. When she knocked, an old woman came out and gave her a heavy jug. She placed the jug in the basket and said, "Porter, take your basket and follow me." The porter followed her to the fruit seller, where she bought red and yellow apples, peaches, lemons, and oranges. She put all of this into the porter's basket and asked him to follow her. He did, crying, "O lucky day, O happy day."

Then she stopped at the butcher's and ordered ten pounds of fresh lamb. She placed this in the basket and said, "Porter, follow me." The porter marveled at all the wonderful things she was buying. Then he placed his basket on his head and followed her to the grocer's, to the bakery, and to the drugstore. She put all of her goods in the basket, turned to the porter, and said, "Take your basket and follow me."

The porter carried the basket and walked behind her until she got to a large house with great pillars and a double door covered with ivory and shining gold. The woman stopped at the door and knocked softly.

But morning drew near Scheherazade, and she fell silent. Dinarzad said to her sister, "Sister, what a strange and amazing story!" Scheherazade replied, "This is nothing compared with what I will tell you tomorrow."

THE NINTH NIGHT

The following night, when Scheherazade was in bed, her sister Dinarzad said, "Please, sister, tell us another of your amazing

tales." The king added, "Let it be the end of the porter's story."
Scheherazade replied, "With the greatest pleasure!"

I heard, O happy King, that as the porter stood with the basket, the door swung open. The porter looked to see who opened the door, and there was another beautiful woman, with a high forehead like the new moon and teeth as white as a row of pearls.

When the porter saw her, he cried, "I have never seen a more blessed day than this!" Then the woman who had opened the door said to the one who had done the shopping, "Sister, what are you waiting for? Come in and let this poor man put down his basket."

The shopper and the porter went in, and the doorkeeper followed them into a grand hall. In the middle stood a large pool of water with a fountain in the center, and at the end was a curtain of red silk. The curtain was pulled open, and from behind it came another dazzling woman with a face brighter than the sun. She walked over to them and said, "Why are you standing? Take the load off this poor man."

The three sisters helped the porter lift the basket down and empty it out. They stacked everything in neat piles and gave the porter a tip.

When the porter saw how charming and beautiful the women were and the many goods they had stacked around them, he did not want to leave. One of the women asked him, "Why don't you go? Is your tip too little?" Then she turned to her sister and said, "Give him more money."

The porter replied, "By God, the money is not too little, but I notice there is no one here to entertain you. A table needs four legs to stand on, and you being three, surely you need a fourth."

When the women heard what he said, they replied, "You are very welcome to join us." Then the three sisters set out all kinds of food and drink by the pool. The porter thought he was in dream. The porter and the women ate and drank and sang, then ate and drank and sang some more. The porter was full of joy. He began dancing and joking, and the three sisters began dancing and joking with him. They passed many hours like this, eating and singing and playing.

But morning drew near Scheherazade, and she fell silent. Dinarzad said to her sister, "Sister, what a strange and lovely story!" Scheherazade replied, "This is nothing compared with what I will tell you tomorrow, if I am still alive."

THE TENTH NIGHT

The following night, when Scheherazade was in bed, her sister Dinarzad said, "Please, sister, tell us more of these lovely tales of yours." The king added, "Let it be the rest of the porter's story." Scheherazade replied, "With the greatest pleasure!"

When it was dark, the three sisters said to the porter, "Sir, it is time for you to get up. Put on your slippers and go." The porter replied, "It would be easier for my soul to leave my body than for me to leave your company. Let us continue as we are and then part ways in the morning."

The shopper said, "Sisters, let him stay, and let's keep having fun." The sisters agreed, but said, "Sir, you must agree to one thing. Get up and go see what is written upon our front door."

He got up, went to the door, and found these words in gold lettering: FOR THOSE WHO MEDDLE IN THE CONCERNS OF OTHERS, THE PUNISHMENT WILL BE GREAT. The porter came back and said, "I promise that I will not ask about what is not my concern."

Then they lit the lamps and spent a long time there laughing and joking and enjoying themselves. Suddenly they heard a knock on the door. One of the women rose, went to the door, and returned after a while, saying, "Sisters, if you listen to me, you will have a delightful night to remember." They asked, "How so?"

She replied, "Three one-eyed dervishes are standing at the door, each with a shaved head and a shaved beard, and each blind in one eye. These religious men have just arrived in Baghdad and have never seen our great city before. Being strangers with nowhere to go, they knocked on our door, hoping we would let them sleep in our stable or offer them a room for the night. Sisters, would you agree to let them in, so that we may amuse ourselves?"

The sisters agreed, saying, "Let them in, but warn them that for those who meddle in the concerns of others, the punishment will be great." The shopper left and returned with the three dervishes, who greeted them and bowed. The other sisters rose to greet them. The women were all delighted at this visit.

When the dervishes saw the beautiful hall full

of food and drink, and the three beautiful sisters, they said all at once, "By God, this is fine." The women laughed and sat down with the porter and the dervishes. They all ate and drank, until the porter said to the dervishes, "Friends, will you entertain us with something?"

But morning drew near Scheherazade, and she fell silent. Dinarzad said to her sister, "Sister, what a strange and amazing story!" Scheherazade replied, "This is nothing compared with what I will tell you tomorrow."

THE ELEVENTH NIGHT

The following night, when Scheherazade was in bed, her sister Dinarzad said, "Please, sister, tell us more of these lovely tales." The king added, "Tell us what happened to the dervishes." Scheherazade replied, "With the greatest pleasure!"

I heard, O King, that three dervishes called for musical instruments, and that the sister who was the doorkeeper brought them a tambourine, a flute, and a harp. The dervishes rose and took the instruments. They tuned them and started to play and sing while the women sang around them until it got very loud. Finally, they heard a heavy knock on the door. The doorkeeper went to see what was the matter.

Now, it happened that the caliph, the great commander of the people, and his vizier Ja'far had come into the city. As they passed by the door, they had heard the sounds of music and laughing.

The caliph said, "Ja'far, I would like to enter this house and visit the people inside." Ja'far replied, "O Prince of the faithful, these people do not know who we are, and I am afraid we will not be welcome." The caliph said, "Don't argue. I must go in." So Ja'far knocked at the door. When the doorkeeper came and opened the door, the vizier stepped forward, kissed the ground before her, and said, "O my lady, we are poor merchants who passed your door. We heard the sounds of music and the noise and hoped that you might let us in and give us shelter for the night."

The doorkeeper felt sorry for them and let them in. When the men entered the hall, the entire group—the girls, the dervishes, and the porter—rose to greet them, and then everyone sat down.

But morning drew near Scheherazade, and she fell silent. Dinarzad said to her sister, "Sister, what a strange and lovely story!" Scheherazade replied, "This is nothing compared with what I will tell you tomorrow, if I am still alive."

THE TWELFTH NIGHT

The following night, when Scheherazade was in bed, her sister Dinarzad said, "Please, tell us another amazing tale." The king added, "Let it be the rest of the story of three sisters." Scheherazade replied, "With the greatest pleasure!"

It is said, O King, that after the caliph and Ja'far entered and sat down, the women turned to them and said, "We are happy to have you as our guests, but you must understand one thing." "What is that thing?" they asked. The girls replied, "For those who meddle in the concerns of others, the punishment will be great."

The men answered, "As you wish. We do not want to pry." Pleased with this response, the sisters sat down to entertain them. They all ate and drank some more, and there was singing and dancing and much carrying-on. The caliph was astonished to see the dervishes, all blind in one eye, and how well they played the flute, the tambourine, and the harp. He was amazed to see three sisters with such beauty, charm, grace, and kindness.

Later in the night, after much more drinking and talking and singing, the sisters rose from their seats. The doorkeeper cleared the table and cleared the middle of the hall. She had the dervishes sit down at one table and the caliph and Ja'far at another.

Then the shopper took out two black dogs, leading them to the middle of the hall. The sisters started dancing as the rest looked on with wonder. The dogs were let loose from their chains, and the sisters danced with the dogs. They spun around and around, until the one of the dogs grew so tired that it fell down from exhaustion. One of the sisters bent down and kissed it on the forehead, and they all danced some more, spinning wildly, until the other dog passed out.

The caliph wanted to know more about what he was seeing, but Ja'far stopped him. "This is not the time to ask questions," he said.

O happy King, when the dancing was done,

the two black dogs were led away again. The sisters came back and moved to couches with their guests. The lamps still glowed, and there was still food and drink, but the men felt astonished and bewildered by the events they had just seen.

But morning drew near Scheherazade, and she fell silent. Dinarzad said to her sister, "What an amazing and entertaining story!" Scheherazade replied, "This is nothing compared with what I will tell you tomorrow, if I live."

THE THIRTEENTH NIGHT

The following night, when Scheherazade was in bed, her sister Dinarzad said, "Please, sister, tell us one of your lovely little tales to pass the night." The king added, "Let it be even more amazing than the last tale." Scheherazade replied, "Very well!"

I heard, O King, that the shopper then got up and left the room. She returned with a yellow-and-green silk bag. She took a lute out of the bag and, plucking the strings, began to sing a sad song. The song was so sad that it moved the doorkeeper to tears. The caliph looked at her and said to Ja'far, "By God, I need to know what has happened here."

Ja'far warned, "My lord, this is not the time. These women made us aware that for those who meddle in the concerns of others, the punishment will be great." But the caliph replied, "By God, I will ask for an explanation of this."

Then the caliph turned to the dervishes and said, "You are members of the household. Perhaps you can explain these strange sights to us." They replied, "We know nothing and we have never laid eyes on this place before tonight. This man beside you should know the answer."

They pointed at the porter, but he replied, "By God, though I have been raised here in Baghdad, never in my life have I entered this house before today." Then the caliph said, "We are six strong men. Will you join with me in demanding an answer for what we have seen here?"

They agreed to proceed—except for Ja'far, who said, "Leave these women alone. We are their guests and, as you know, we made a promise." Then he whispered to the caliph, "Leave them this one last hour of the night, and tomorrow morning I will come back and bring them before you to tell their story."

But the caliph yelled at him, "I can no longer wait! Let the dervishes question them." Ja'far replied, "This is not a good idea." The two men shouted and argued.

When the girls heard the noise they were making, one of them asked, "What is the matter?" The porter came up to her and said, "My lady, these men wish for you to tell them your story and explain the strange things that have gone on here tonight."

Turning to the room, the woman asked, "Is it true what he says?" The visitors replied, "Yes"—except for Ja'far, who kept silent. When the sisters heard this reply, one of them said, "O friends, you have offended us. Have we not told you of our condition, that 'he who speaks of what does not concern him will hear that which will not please him'? We took you into our home and fed you with our food, but after all of this you did us wrong."

Then she struck the floor three times, crying out, "Come at once." A door opened and out came six men with swords in their hands. In no time, these men had the guests tied by the hands and feet and bound to one another. Then they led them to the center of the hall, and one man stood by each of the guests with his sword drawn above the guest's head. They said, "O most honorable ladies, permit us to strike off their heads." One of the sisters replied, "Wait a minute while I question them." The porter cried out, "God protect me. O lady, do not kill me for another man's sins!" Then he began to weep and cry and beg.

The woman laughed. She came up to the group and said to the men with swords, "Whoever tells us his tale and explains what has happened to him and what has brought him to this place, let him go. But whoever refuses, strike off his head."

But morning drew near Scheherazade, and she fell into silence. Dinarzad said to her sister, "What an amazing and entertaining story!" Scheherazade replied, "This is nothing compared with what I will tell you tomorrow, if I live."

THE FOURTEENTH NIGHT

The following night, Dinarzad said, "Please, sister, tell us more of this amazing tale." The king added, "Tell us what happened to the six guests." Scheherazade replied, "Very well!"

I heard, O King, that the first to come forth was the porter, who said, "Mistress, you know the reason that I came to this place was that I was hired by this woman, who led me from one store to the next and finally to this house. This is my tale." The woman replied, "You may go." But he replied, "By God, I will stay until I hear the tales of the others."

CHAPTER 4

The First Dervish's Tale

Then the first dervish came forward and said:

My lady, the cause of my eye being lost and my beard being shaved off is this: My father was a king, and he had a brother who was also a king and had a son and a daughter. As the years went by, I used to visit my uncle every now and then. Between my uncle's son and myself, there grew a great friendship.

One day, I visited my cousin, and he treated me with unusual kindness. He prepared a great feast, and after we ate and drank our fill, he said, "Cousin I would like to show you something, but you must keep it a secret." I replied, "With the greatest pleasure." After he had me take an oath, he said, "Come with me."

I followed him to a graveyard, where we came before a great tomb. My cousin broke open the wall of the tomb, setting the stones to the side, and I followed him inside. He showed me an iron plate the size of a small door. He raised the plate and revealed a winding staircase. Then he said to me, "Cousin, there is one last favor I have to ask you. After I go down into this place, set the iron plate back over me."

After I followed his instructions, I left and spent the rest of the night at my uncle's house. When I woke up the next morning and remembered the events of the night before, I thought it was all a dream. I asked about my cousin, but no one could tell me anything. Then I went to the graveyard and looked for the tomb, but it had disappeared. I spent a restless night back at my uncle's house and almost went insane with worry, but I had given my word not to say anything about what I had seen. Finally, I decided to go back to my father's city.

As soon as I arrived within the city gates, I was grabbed, beaten, and chained. My father's vizier had plotted against him and taken control of the city. His men carried me before the vizier, who was a great enemy of mine. He burned my eye to punish me, and then ordered one my father's swordsman to take me out into the woods and kill me. The man followed the vizier's orders. He tied me to the back of a horse and led me out into the wilderness. Finally, he went to kill me, and I started weeping bitterly over what had happened. He began weep to with me.

The swordsman felt pity for me and set me free, saying, "Run for your life and never return to this land, for they will kill you and kill me with you." Hardly believing my luck, I kissed his hand, and thought that losing my eye was better than losing my life.

I traveled back to my uncle's city and told him about my father's betrayal. He said to me, "I, too, have great sadness. My son is missing and I do not know what has happened to him." Then he wept. I was unable to remain silent and told him the whole story of what I had seen and done. I saw the king's sorrow turn to rage, which surprised me greatly.

But morning drew near Scheherazade, and she fell silent. Dinarzad said to her sister, "Sister, what an amazing story!" Scheherazade replied, "This is nothing compared with what I will tell you tomorrow, if I live."

THE FIFTEENTH NIGHT

The following night, when Scheherazade was in bed, her sister Dinarzad said, "Please, sister, tell us more of this amazing

tale." The king added, "Let it be the rest of the first dervish's
tale." Scheherazade replied, "Very well!"

I heard, O happy King, that the first dervish said
to the woman:

My lady, when I saw that look on my uncle's face,
I felt terrible, and I said, "For God's sake, Uncle,
don't make me feel worse. I feel sorry enough for
what has happened to your son." He replied,
"Nephew, know that this son of mine was madly
in love with a demon, and I often forbade him
from seeing her, but he did not listen to me and
now I see how he planned everything behind my
back. He built a secret dwelling under the tomb
you speak of and went to meet his demon lover
there. Now I have lost him."

Then we both wept. He looked at me and said,
"You are my son in his place." But there was
hardly time for weeping before we heard the

banging of drums, the sounds of trumpets, and the screaming of men giving orders for battle. We asked what was happening and were told that the vizier who had disposed of my father was now attacking the city with such mighty force, no one could resist him.

It was a terrible battle that followed, and I just managed to escape. I knew that if I fell into the vizier's hands, he would kill both me and my father's swordsman, who had saved my life. My sorrows were greater than ever.

I could think of no way to escape but by shaving my beard and eyebrows to change how I looked, and so that is what I did. Pretending to be a dervish, I left the city, undetected by anyone, with the intention of reaching Baghdad. I was hoping that I might find someone who would assist me to the caliph, the leader of all faithful souls, so that I might tell him my tale. I arrived this very night, and as I stood by the city gate, not knowing where I should go, this dervish by my side came over and greeted me. As we were talking, this other dervish joined us at the gate. The three of us walked until God led us to your home and you were kind enough to let us in.

The woman said, "Rise, you may go." He replied, "By God, I will not go until I hear the tales of the others."

But morning drew near Scheherazade, and she fell silent. Dinarzad said to her sister, "Sister, what an amazing story!" Scheherazade replied, "This is nothing compared with what I will tell you tomorrow, if the king lets me live."

CHAPTER 5

The Second Dervish's Tale

∽

THE SIXTEENTH NIGHT

The following night, when Scheherazade was in bed, her sister Dinarzad said, "Please, sister, tell us one of your lovely little tales." The king added, "Let it be more amazing than what came before." Scheherazade replied, "With the greatest pleasure!"

It is said, O happy King, that everyone was amazed at the tale of the first dervish. The caliph said to Ja'far, "In all my life, I have never heard such a tale." Then the second dervish came forward and said:

By God, my lady, I was not born one-eyed. My father was a king and he taught me how to write and read, and I turned to the study of calligraphy. I perfected my art until word of my skill spread to every town and reached all the great kings.

One day, the king of India sent my father gifts and asked him to send me to him. My father prepared me for the trip with six riding horses. We rode for a full month until one day we came upon a cloud of dust. When the dust cleared, we saw fifty horsemen shining like steel lions in their armor.

They were bandits. We said to them, "We are messengers to the great king of India. You must not harm us." Still, they attacked. I barely escaped alive, wandering off without knowing which direction to go. I had been mighty and rich, but then I became poor.

For a month, I traveled during the day, sleeping at night wherever I could, and eating the plants and fruits of the earth to survive. Finally, I arrived at a beautiful city, weak from exhaustion and hunger. I entered the city, not knowing where to go, and was lucky to pass a tailor sitting in his shop. I greeted him, and he invited me in. I told him everything that had happened to me. He looked troubled and told me, "Young man, do not tell your secret to anyone, for the king of this city is your father's greatest enemy." Then he brought me some food and we ate together. When it was dark, he let me sleep in a small space behind his shop.

I stayed there for three weeks. Then he asked me, "Don't you have any skill to earn your living with?" I replied that I was a writer, and he said

"Such skills are not much in demand in this city. Take an ax and a rope and go cut wood in the wilderness for your living." Then he brought me an ax and a rope and put me under the charge of some woodcutters. I went out with them, cut wood all day long, and came back, carrying my bundle on my head. I sold the wood and brought the money to the tailor. In this way, I spent an entire year.

One day, I went out into the wilderness and came to a thick patch of trees. There was a great stump there, and when I dug around it with my ax, I came upon a ring attached to a wooden plank. I pulled the ring to raise the plank and found a staircase. I went down the steps and found a grand underground palace. Down there was a girl who looked as bright as the shining sun and whose voice chased all sorrow away.

But morning drew near Scheherazade, and she fell silent. Dinarzad said to her sister, "Sister, what an amazing story!"

Scheherazade replied, "It is nothing compared with what I will tell you tomorrow, if the king lets me live."

THE SEVENTEENTH NIGHT

The following night, when Scheherazade was in bed, her sister Dinarzad said, "Please, sister, tell us more of this lovely tale." The king added, "Let it be the rest of the second dervish's tale." Scheherazade replied, "Very well!"

I heard, O happy king, that the second dervish said:

When the girl saw me, she asked, "What are you, a man or a demon?" I replied, "I am a man." She asked, "What brought you here? I have lived in this place for twenty-five years without ever seeing another person."

I replied, "My good fortune brought me here to take away your sorrows." Then I told my story to her, and she felt sad for me and told me her story as well. She was the daughter of a king from a distant island. On the night of her wedding, a demon flew away with her and set her down in that place. Once every ten days, he visited her, and the rest of the time she was alone. If she needed the demon, all she had to do was touch two lines engraved on the doorway.

The demon was not due for six more days, and so I stayed there with the princess. I soon fell in love, and said to her, "My beautiful one, let me carry you up and save you from this prison." She replied, "O, be still. The demon is frightening and I am afraid to leave him."

I grew very angry then and said, "This very instant, I will smash the engraved inscription and let the demon come, so that I may destroy him!" When she heard my words, the princess grew pale and said, "No, for God's sake, don't do it."

But I was too angry to listen, and I kicked the door with my foot.

But morning drew near Scheherazade, and she fell silent. Dinarzad said to her sister, "Sister, what a wonderful and amazing story!" Scheherazade replied, "It is nothing compared with what I will tell you tomorrow, if the king lets me live."

THE EIGHTEENTH NIGHT

The following night, when Scheherazade was in bed, her sister Dinarzad said, "Please, sister, tell us more of this amazing tale." The king added, "Let it be the end of the second dervish's tale." Scheherazade replied, "With the greatest pleasure!"

It is said, O happy King, that the second dervish said to the woman:

As soon as I kicked the step, there was thunder and lightning and the earth began to shake and everything turned dark.

The princess cried out, "Get up and run for your life." I fled up the staircase, but in my great terror I left my sandals and ax behind. I had almost reached the top when I saw the palace floor split open and the demon appear. When I reached the outside, I replaced the trapdoor as it was before and covered it with earth. I was very sorry as I thought of the princess, who had lived quietly and peacefully for twenty-five years before I disturbed her. I blamed myself for what I had done.

I walked on until I came to my friend the tailor. He was worried and had been waiting for me. He was glad to see me. I thanked him and went to my little room behind the shop.

A bit later, the tailor came to see me and said, "There is an old gentleman waiting outside who has your ax and sandals and is looking for you."

When I heard this, I started to tremble. While we were talking, the wall split open and the old gentleman was there. It was the demon.

But morning drew near Scheherazade, and she fell silent.
Dinarzad said to her sister, "Sister, what an amusing story!"
Scheherazade replied, "It is nothing compared with what I will
tell you tomorrow, if the king lets me live."

THE NINETEENTH NIGHT

The following night, when Scheherazade was in bed, her sister
Dinarzad said, "Please, sister, tell more of this amazing tale."
The king added, "Let it be the rest of the second dervish's
story." Scheherazade replied, "With the greatest pleasure!"

I heard, O happy King, that the second dervish
told the woman:

Then the demon rose up and he was terrible. He
had a mighty sword in his hands, and he held it
up to strike me down. I begged and pleaded with
him for my life, telling him that he had no reason
to kill me.

"You are the man who visited my palace in the woods and who took my woman for your own," he cried.

I told him he was wrong, that I had never seen such a palace or such a woman. I begged and pleaded for a long time until finally he put down his sword.

"I will not kill you," said the demon, "but I will not let you go unharmed." Then he snatched me up and flew with me upward until the earth looked like a distant cloud. Soon he sat me down on a mountain. He took a little dust, mumbled a spell, and at that very instant I turned into an ape. Then the demon flew away.

When I saw that I was an ape, I cried and I felt sorry for myself. I went down from the mountain and walked for a month. I crossed a desert until I got to the shore. I stood there, looking out at the ocean, until I saw the shape of a ship. It got closer and closer. It looked as if it would pass right by me.

I waved to the ship, running back and forth with a branch in my hand.

When the sailors saw me, they said to the captain, "You have risked our lives for an ape? Let us kill him."

When I heard what they said, I got to knees and begged for my life. Then the captain said, "This ape has asked me for help. No one will harm him while he is under my care." He took me onto the ship and treated me kindly.

For fifty days, the ship sailed under a good wind until we got to a great city. No sooner had we docked than we were visited by messengers from the king of the city.

"Good sailors," the messengers said, "our king sends you this piece of paper, and asks each of you write one line on it. A wise man and a great calligrapher has died and the king will only replace him with someone who can write as well as he could."

Then they handed the sailors a roll of paper, and each of them took a turn writing out a line. When they came to me, I snatched the roll from their hands and they screamed at me, fearing that I would throw it into the sea or tear it into pieces. But I showed them that I only wanted to write on it.

They were quite amazed by this, but the captain said, "Let him write what he likes, and if he writes well I will adopt him for my son, because I have never seen a more intelligent or well-behaved ape."

Then I held the pen, dipped it in the ink, and wrote some

lines. I handed them the roll and they took it back in amazement.

But morning drew near Scheherazade, and she fell silent. Dinarzad said to her sister, "Sister, what an amazing story!" Scheherazade replied, "It is nothing compared with what I will tell you tomorrow, if the king lets me live."

THE TWENTIETH NIGHT

The following night, when Scheherazade was in bed, her sister Dinarzad said, "Please, sister, tell us more of this lovely tale." The king added, "Make it the end of the second dervish's story." Scheherazade replied, "Very well!"

It is told, O happy king, that the second dervish said to the woman:

The messengers took the scroll and returned with it to the king. My writing pleased him, and he said, "Take this robe of honor to the person who wrote these lines."

The men smiled and said, "O King of the age and the world, the writer of these lines is an ape." The king asked, "Is it true?" They told him it was, and the king was greatly amazed. Then he said, "I wish to see this ape." He sent his messengers to me, and they dressed me with the robe of honor and took me to him.

When I saw the king, I bowed down three times before him. Then I kissed the ground once, and he noted my fine manners. "This is a wonder," said the king, and he ordered a table of food set before him. He asked me to eat with him. I ate only a little before writing out some more lines for him.

The king read what I wrote and said, "If a man had this skill, he would pass all other men."

Just then, the king's daughter appeared. She wore a veil on her face. "O Father," she said, "do you think so little of me that you would expose me to this man?" The king was astonished and said, "Daughter, there is no one here but this ape. Why do you veil your face?" She replied, "An ape? Why, this is a wise and kind man, put under a spell by a demon."

Then the king turned to his daughter and said, "How do you know this?" She replied, "O Father, I have copied and learned a hundred books of spells. I could move the stones of your city into the ocean and even beyond the ends of the earth. I could make the sky darken, turning day into night, for a hundred days."

The king said, "O daughter, free this ape from his spell, so that I may make him my vizier and allow him to marry you." She replied, "As you wish."

The king's daughter began to whisper a spell and then ordered a bowl of water. She sprinkled me with the water and said, "I command you to be yourself again."

Suddenly I stood before her as a man. But there was little time for joy. In a flash the demon appeared in the sky, taking the form of a terrible lion. We were terrified. The world turned dark all around us.

The demon cursed the princess for what she had done. She answered him by turning into a great serpent and flying into the air. There was an incredible battle that shook the castle under our feet. The fight lasted for some time, with the girl and the demon taking the shapes of different animals. Finally, there was the sound of a great explosion. A bright light flashed in the sky.

It was this light that blinded me in one eye. The floor shook beneath me, and I could see that the walls of the palace were crumbling. I ran as fast as I could, barely escaping before the entire palace collapsed.

I left the palace ruins, my heart heavy with sadness. I went to shave my beard and eyebrows so as to look like a dervish. I traveled through many countries, my sorrow growing worse and worse. I hoped to find the caliph, so that I might tell him my tale. I arrived here this night and met these men at the city gates. This is my story, and such is the reason for my losing an eye and shaving my beard.

The woman replied, "You may go." But he replied, "By God, I will stay until I hear the tales of the others."

But morning drew near Scheherazade, and she fell silent. Dinarzad said to her sister, "Sister, what an amazing story!" Scheherazade replied, "It is nothing compared with what I will tell you tomorrow, if the king lets me live."

CHAPTER 6

The Third Dervish's Tale

⌒ღ

THE TWENTY-FIRST NIGHT

The following night, when Scheherazade was in bed, her sister
Dinarzad said, "Please, sister, tell us another of your lovely
little tales." The king added, "Let it be the last dervish's tale."
Scheherazade replied, "With the greatest pleasure!"

I heard, O King, that the third dervish said to the
woman:

My story is stranger and more amazing than the
other dervishes' tales, and yet I brought my misery

upon myself. My father was a great king, and when he died, I inherited his kingdom. I was quite wealthy and powerful, but one day I decided to travel to some distant islands. My crew loaded my boats with a month's supply of goods, and we set sail. Soon we came to an island that seemed quite pleasant. Here we landed and prepared some food. We rested for a few days and then set out to sea again.

We sailed for a dozen days but, as we sailed, the sea kept growing before us and the land got smaller behind us. The lookout came down to me and said, "I looked to the right and there is nothing but sky and water, and I looked to the left and saw something great and black in the distance."

When the captain heard this, he threw his turban down on the deck and began to cry and pull his hair out. I asked him what had happened.

He replied, "O King, we are all going to perish. The storm is driving us toward a fate we cannot escape. By midday tomorrow, we will reach a black mountain of metal. This mountain has a great power to attract metal. When any ship passes by it, every nail will fly to the mountain, and the ship's sides will come apart. O King, at the top of the mountain, there is a brass horse with a brass horseman. While the mountain destroys the ship, this horseman destroys the people who come there."

The next day, we passed by the mountain. Just as the captain had said, the mountain pulled the nails out of the ship and the ship fell apart. God spared me, and I was able to cling to one of the planks from the ship. I floated, ending up at the foot of the terrible island, where I saw a staircase carved out of rock.

I began to climb this staircase, calling on God to protect me. I reached the top of the mountain and came to a great brass dome not far from where the horseman stood. I said my prayers there, thanking God for saving me, and fell asleep overlooking the sea.

In a dream, I heard a voice that said, "When you wake from your sleep, dig beneath your feet. You will find a brass bow with three arrows. Use these to shoot the brass horseman off his horse and rid the earth of this monster. He will fall into the sea, and the water will swell to the level of the dome. A small boat will come, and you must paddle this boat for ten days until it takes you to safety. However, you must not call out the name of God. If you do, you will not be saved."

I woke up and did just as the voice said. After the horseman fell into the sea, the waters rose, and the small boat appeared. I rowed for nine days, until I saw the shapes of hills in the distance. I was so joyful that I prayed, calling out, "There is none greater than God."

Just then the boat turned over and sank into the sea. I swam for three days but there was no land near me. I was sure I would drown, but then a sudden gust of wind blew over me, and a great wave carried me to the shores of an island.

But morning drew near Scheherazade, and she fell silent. Dinarzad said to her sister, "Sister, what an amazing story!" Scheherazade replied, "This is nothing compared with what I will tell you tomorrow, if the king lets me live."

THE TWENTY-SECOND NIGHT

The following night, when Scheherazade was in bed, her sister Dinarzad said, "Please, sister, tell us more of this amazing tale." The king added, "Let it be the rest of the third dervish's tale." Scheherazade replied, "With the greatest pleasure!"

It is said, O happy King, that the third dervish continued:

There was a huge mountain on this island, and I climbed until I reached the top of it. There was a great palace covered with red gold. The door stood open, and I entered. I found a beautiful hall filled with forty girls, dressed in silk gowns with glittering jewels. They rushed to me and brought me to a comfortable chair. They washed my hands and feet and brought me food and drink. The forty girls sat around me, talking and laughing.

I forgot all my miseries then and thought, "This is the best of life, which sadly is so short." I spent a whole year in that beautiful palace, eating, drinking, and enjoying all of life. When the new year came, the girls began weeping, clinging to me, and saying, "May you never leave." I asked why they were weeping and why they thought I was leaving.

"You yourself will be the cause," they replied. They told me that they were the forty daughters of forty kings, and that once a year they had to leave the palace for forty days. When they left, I had to stay behind. I could eat and drink and do as I pleased, looking around in every room of the house but the one with the door of red gold.

"And this is how you will disobey us," they said. "When you open this door, it will cause our separation."

They left then, and I said, "By God, I will never open that door." I was alone in that place for thirty-nine days, and for thirty-nine days I ate and drank as I pleased, exploring every room but the one with the door of red gold. All the rooms were full of fabulous delights such as fruit trees and gardens of fragrant flowers. As the thirty-nine days passed, though, I became more and more curious about what was in the room with door of red gold. Finally, I couldn't control myself, and I opened the door. Inside, there were lamps of gold and silver and the strong smell of perfume.

Standing in the middle of the room was a horse as black as the deepest night. Amazed at the beauty of this creature, I led him outside the palace. I tried to ride him, but he would not move. Finally I hit the horse, and he roared with anger. Revealing a pair of wings, he flew up with me, high into the sky. He traveled with me a great distance before throwing me off his back. He lashed my face with his tail, making me blind in one eye, and dropped me in a lonely desert.

I was full of misery, and walked for days and days, cursing myself for my actions. When I came to a city, I shaved off my beard like a dervish and kept walking. I roamed the world before I reached Baghdad. That is how I met these two dervishes and how I came here. And this is the story of how I lost my eye and shaved off my beard.

The woman replied, "You may go."

Then the three dervishes came together and

said, "O our lady and mistress, we wish you to grant us our lives and to let us leave here."

The woman replied, "I will." When they were all outside, the caliph revealed himself to the dervishes. They fell to their knees before him, giving thanks to God. He took the men home with him, granting them the safety and refuge in his palace. The dervishes rejoiced that they had found the caliph, confident that he would help deliver them from their misery.

But morning drew near Scheherazade, and she fell silent. Dinarzad said to her sister, "Sister, what an amazing story!" Scheherazade replied, "This is nothing compared with what I will tell you tomorrow, if the king lets me live."

CHAPTER 7

The Tale of Sinbad the Sailor and Sinbad the Porter

c⊙

THE TWENTY-THIRD NIGHT

The following night, when Scheherazade was in bed, her sister Dinarzad said, "Please, sister, tell us one of your lovely little tales." The king added, "Let it be even more amazing than the last." Scheherazade replied, "With the greatest pleasure!"

It is said, O great King, that in Baghdad there was a poor porter named Sinbad. One day, he set his load of goods down before the gates of a rich merchant. From inside, he heard the sounds of lutes playing and people dancing and eating. Sinbad prayed to God, cursing his misery and complaining about his poor luck in life. Just as he had finished his prayer, the gates swung open. Sinbad walked in. He saw a beautiful house, like none he had seen before. The merchant welcomed him kindly, asking his name.

"My name is Sinbad the Porter," he replied. The host said, "My name is the same, for I am called Sinbad the Sailor." Then he asked the porter to sit down, and Sinbad the Sailor told him of his voyages and the many dangers he had faced:

My father was a rich man and left me a lot of money. But it did not help me. I wasted the money away until there was hardly anything left. I took what remained and bought goods to take on a trading voyage at sea. We passed from island to island and finally came to one that was just as beautiful as paradise itself. We had just started a fire for cooking when I heard the captain crying, "Run! In the name of God, run for the ship!"

We all ran, not knowing then that the whole island was actually a giant fish. We were too late. Some made it to the ship, but others of us were tossed into the wild ocean by the jerking and shaking of the fish. The strong tide soon pulled me to an island, where I landed on the beach.

Looking around, I spotted a beautiful horse tied to a tree by the shore. As I was walked over to the horse, the ground split open and a man came out. He asked me what my story was. When I told him, he led me downstairs, beneath the earth, where he gave me food and drink. He told a peculiar tale. He was the servant of a great king who sent him here at every new moon and ordered him to tie his horse by the shore. Each time, the waves of the sea would wash up near the mare.

The servant would untie the horse and watch her plunge wildly into the sea. When the mare returned from the sea, she would be pregnant. Later, she would deliver a colt worth a great deal of money.

I was amazed at this story, but I went along with the servant, and everything he had spoken of came true. Then the servant brought me to the other side of island and introduced me to his king, who treated me kindly and put me to work meeting ships as they came into the port. I lived this way for many months before a familiar ship arrived. The sailors aboard said that the owner had died, and I asked them for his name. "Sinbad," they replied. I told them I was the man they spoke of. Looking again, they recognized me and welcomed me with open arms.

The ship had made a lot of money from selling my goods, and I gave some of it to the king to thank him. Then I sailed home, richer than ever before. I promised never to take such a voyage again.

But morning drew near Scheherazade, and she fell silent. Dinarzad said to her sister, "Sister, what an amazing story!" Scheherazade replied, "It is nothing compared with what I will tell you tomorrow, if the king lets me live."

THE TWENTY-FOURTH NIGHT

The following night, when Scheherazade was in bed, her sister Dinarzad said, "Please, sister, tell us another of your lovely little tales." The king added, "Let it be more amazing than the last." Scheherazade replied, "As you wish!"

It is said, O happy King, that after hearing the story, Sinbad the Porter thanked his host and prepared to leave. Sinbad the Sailor invited him to return the next day and dine with him again.

So the porter returned to the house the next day. Once more, the gates swung open, and once more he found people eating and dancing inside the beautiful home. Sinbad the Sailor welcomed him kindly, asked him to sit, and gave him food and drink. Then the sailor resumed the tale of his adventures and the many great dangers he had faced:

After I had been at home some years, I desired to travel again. I bought goods and set out on a trading voyage with a number of merchants. We came to a lovely and deserted island and stopped for a while there. I fell asleep. Later I woke with terror to find that the ship was gone.

Climbing a tall tree, I saw a giant bird, twice the size of an elephant, whose wings could block out the sun. When the great bird flew over me, I grabbed its leg, hoping to escape. I held on until it took me near a high hill. Then I let go.

I went down the hill and found myself in a valley full of diamonds. But it was also crawling with snakes. I hid from the snakes in a cave, but I could not sleep well, for there was a terrible snake in there as well, guarding its eggs. I was scared it would eat me.

The next morning, I crept outside. Suddenly a huge piece of meat fell down from the sky in front of me. I had heard of this place and knew there was a trick the merchants used here. They would throw the meat into the valley, hoping that the diamonds would stick to it. They knew the eagles and vultures would soon attack the meat and fly up to the mountaintops with it in their claws. Then the merchants would scare the birds away and take the diamonds.

Quickly I filled my pockets with diamonds and used some rope to tie myself to the meat. An eagle swooped down and carried me up to the top of a mountain. There a man jumped out, shouting at the eagle until it flew away.

The man was surprised when he saw me there, but I gave him some of the diamonds and told him my story. He brought me to some of his merchant friends, and they were all amazed at the story I told. I was able to trade my diamonds for some goods and a ship to take me home. There I swore never to take another sea voyage again.

Sinbad the Porter marveled at this tale. He thanked Sinbad, his host, and prepared to leave. The sailor and merchant invited him to return the next day and dine with them again.

But morning drew near Scheherazade, and she fell silent. Dinarzad said to her sister, "Sister, what an amazing story!" Scheherazade replied, "It is nothing compared with what I will tell you tomorrow, if the king lets me live."

THE TWENTY-FIFTH NIGHT

The following night, when Scheherazade was in bed, her sister Dinarzad said, "Please, sister, tell us one of your lovely little tales." The king added, "Let it be even more amazing than the last." Scheherazade replied, "With the greatest pleasure!"

It is said O, happy King, that the porter returned to the house the next day. Once more, the gates swung open, and once more he found people eating and dancing inside the beautiful home. Sinbad the Sailor welcomed him kindly, asked him to sit, and gave him food and drink. Then the sailor resumed the tale of his adventures and the many great dangers he had faced:

After being home awhile, I once again wanted to travel. I bought goods for trading and set out on a sea voyage with a group of merchants. We traveled from island to island, trading our goods. One day, a great wind carried us to an island with many mountains. On the island lived large, hairy beasts that looked like apes. These animals grabbed the cables of our ship, ripping them apart with their teeth. They dragged us to the shore and ran off with all our food.

We roamed around the island, cursing our poor luck. Finally, we came to a great castle with a large courtyard. We were tired from our walking and quickly fell asleep there.

Later, we were woken by a terrible rumbling. The earth shook beneath us, and a horrible creature came down to us from the castle. He was shaped like a man but much taller, with eyes like glowing coals, tusks like a boar, and terrible claws like a lion.

All of us were shaking with fear. Many of the men tried to run, but I could not escape. The creature scooped me up and looked at me to see if I would be good for eating. After finding me too skinny, the creature tossed me aside and grabbed one of the other men, then tossed him aside, too. He treated us all like this until he finally picked up the captain. Then he tucked the captain under his arm and went back into the castle.

We spent the day looking for a place to hide from this monster, but we could not escape. The next morning, he returned and took away another man. We knew that soon he would take all of us. We had to do everything we could to escape.

The following day, we made a simple boat and filled it with whatever food we could find. Returning to the castle walls, we built a fire and heated up two iron rods until they were white hot. When the monster returned that night, we surprised him and blinded him with the two rods.

There came a terrible roaring that shook the earth. The monster groped around looking for us. But he could not see us, and we made our escape, pushing off in the boat and making it safely out to sea. The monster tried to follow, wading into the water and throwing great rocks into the ocean.

We sailed to an island where we were met by other ships with merchants trading goods. One of the captains felt pity for me and offered me the goods of a lost merchant named Sinbad. I marveled at this news and revealed to the men my identity, and that this was my very own ship.

I sailed on, going from island to island and selling what goods were left. I saw many amazing things along the way, including a fish shaped like a cow and a bird that hatched from a seashell. At last, I returned home and held a great feast to forget my hardships. I promised never to go on a sea voyage again.

Sinbad the Porter marveled at this tale. He thanked his host and prepared to leave. Sinbad the Sailor invited him to return the next day and join their dinner again.

But morning drew near Scheherazade, and she fell silent. Dinarzad said to her sister, "Sister, what an amazing story!" Scheherazade replied, "This is nothing compared with what I will tell you tomorrow, if the king lets me live."

THE TWENTY-SIXTH NIGHT

The following night, when Scheherazade was in bed, her sister Dinarzad said, "Please, sister, tell us one of your lovely little tales." The king added, "Let it be the rest of the tale of Sinbad." Scheherazade replied, "With the greatest pleasure!"

It is said, O happy King, that the porter returned to the house the next day. Once more, the gates swung open, and once more he found a good number of people eating and dancing inside the beautiful home. Sinbad the Sailor welcomed him kindly, asked him to sit, and gave him food and drink. Then the sailor resumed the tale of his adventures and the many great dangers he had faced:

I settled quite happily at home and lived there for many years. But one day, I heard some merchants discussing plans for a sea voyage. I decided to set sail with them. We had been at sea for only a couple of days when a powerful storm cast us all overboard. The waves washed us onto a small island.

We looked up to see a number of men coming toward us. They carried us to a great house and brought us before their king. A meal was set before us, and we started eating. The food looked odd, though, and I saw that the king did not eat any. So I only pretended to eat it, although my companions ate greedily. Soon they were acting strangely and talking nonsense. That night I went to bed still hungry.

Every day, the king set out tables full of the odd food, and every day I pretended to eat. I grew thinner and thinner; meanwhile, my friends grew fatter and acted more and more foolishly. Seeing this, I started to think that the king was fattening us up so that he could eat us. I was so terrified that, abandoning my companions, I ran off and hid in the woods for many days, hungry and tired. I ate plants to stay alive and finally made it to the far shore of the island. There I saw a ship and waved at it.

The ship came near and I swam out to it, escaping the terrible island. I returned home with as much of my wealth as I could keep on me, and whenever I think of that place I nearly pass out at the horror of it.

Sinbad the Porter marveled at this tale. He thanked his host and prepared to leave. Sinbad the Sailor invited him to return the next day and join their dinner again.

But morning drew near Scheherazade, and she fell silent. Dinarzad said to her sister, "Sister, what an amazing story!" Scheherazade replied, "This is nothing compared with what I will tell you tomorrow, if the king lets me live."

THE TWENTY-SEVENTH NIGHT

The following night, when Scheherazade was in bed, her sister Dinarzad said, "Please, sister, tell us one of your amazing tales. The king added, "Let it be the rest of the tale of Sinbad." Scheherazade replied, "With the greatest pleasure!"

It is said O, happy King, that Sinbad the Porter returned to the house the next day. Once more, the gates swung open, and once more he found people eating and dancing inside the beautiful home. Sinbad the Sailor welcomed him kindly, asked him to sit, and gave him food and drink. Then the sailor resumed the tale of his adventures and the many great dangers he had faced:

Though I said I would never leave my home again, I set out for the fifth time on a sea voyage in a tall ship full of goods to trade.

After sailing for a few days, my crew and I saw a huge white dome on an island. We sailed toward it and docked by the shore. It was an egg, and we cracked it open with stones to see what was inside. Just as we had opened it, the sky became dark. A huge bird flew over, and its large wings blocked out the sun. We knew it must be the mother, so we hurried back to the ship and off to sea. But the mother bird dropped giant rocks on us and broke our ship to pieces. I grabbed hold of a plank of wood and was washed ashore on a beautiful island.

I explored the island, hoping to find some food, when I came upon an old man sitting by a stream. He asked me to carry him across to the other side, and I agreed to do so. He climbed on my shoulders and clamped his legs around my neck. He held so tight to me that I nearly choked, and I could not get him off of me.

The old man forced me to carry him around the island all night and day, with hardly a rest. One day we found some grapes, which made the old man quite happy. I told him that I could make the grapes into a drink for him, and he was delighted at this.

When the mixture was ready, the old man drank it down like water. He grew quite merry and soon fell asleep. I escaped from him easily and made my way down to the shore. A passing ship picked me up, and I told the sailors my story. They were amazed to hear my tale. They said the old man I had met was the Old Man of the Sea, and that no one had ever escaped from him.

We sailed to an island rich in spices. I managed to buy a great number of goods here. I returned home and sold my spices for a lot of money.

Sinbad the Porter marveled at this tale. He thanked his host and prepared to leave. Sinbad the Sailor invited him to return the next day and join their dinner again.

But morning drew near Scheherazade, and she fell silent. Dinarzad said to her sister, "Sister, what an amazing story!" Scheherazade replied, "This is nothing compared with what I will tell you tomorrow, if the king lets me live."

THE TWENTY-EIGHTH NIGHT

The following night, when Scheherazade was in bed, her sister Dinarzad said, "Please, sister, tell us one of your lovely tales."

The king added, "Tell us the rest of Sinbad's story."
Scheherazade replied, "With the greatest pleasure!"

It is said, O happy King, that the porter returned
to the house the next day. Once more, the gates
swung open, and once more he found people eating and dancing inside the beautiful home.
Sinbad the Sailor welcomed him kindly, asked
him to sit, and gave him food and drink. Then the
sailor resumed the tale of his adventures and the
many great dangers he had faced:

I soon wanted to travel again. I purchased goods
and joined a group of merchants setting out on a
sea voyage. But our ship was wrecked on an
island, and only a few of us survived.

We climbed the great cliffs of the island and
were nearly driven mad by what we saw there.
The island's streams were full of jewels, and its
trees were made of emerald and jade. The great

riches dazzled us, but there was nothing to eat or drink. Weeks passed, and I was the only one left alive. I was full of sadness, and dug my grave by the sea. I prepared to lie in it and let wind blow sand over me.

Just then I saw some planks of wood that had washed from our ship up onto the shore. I used this wood to build a raft, which I filled with jewels. I paddled the raft out to sea, but I was so tired and hungry that I soon passed out. When I woke up, the raft was tied to an island, and I looked up to see a tribe of men standing over me. They gave me food and drink, and I told them of my adventures. Afterward, they brought me to their king.

I presented the king some of the jewels I had gathered and repeated for him my story about the land where I had come from. Very much amazed, the king prepared a ship full of his merchants to sail that way for trading. I was allowed to sail with them, and so I found my way home again. I still had plenty of the jewels with me and returned much richer than I had ever been before.

Sinbad the Porter marveled at this tale. He thanked his host and prepared to leave. Sinbad the Sailor invited him to return the next day and join their dinner again.

But morning drew near Scheherazade, and she fell silent. Dinarzad said to her sister, "Sister, what an amazing story!" Scheherazade replied, "It is nothing compared with what I will tell you tomorrow, if the king lets me live."

THE THIRTIETH NIGHT

The following night, when Scheherazade was in bed, her sister Dinarzad said, "Please, sister, tell us more of this tale." The king added, "Let it be the rest of the story of Sinbad." Scheherazade replied, "With the greatest pleasure!"

It is said, O happy King, that the porter returned to the house the next day. Once more, the gates swung open, and once more he found people eating and dancing inside the beautiful home. Sinbad the Sailor welcomed him kindly, asked him to sit, and gave him food and drink. Then the sailor resumed the tale of his adventures and the many great dangers he had faced:

After my last voyage, I promised never again to leave my home. But the desire to travel was too strong, and I shipped out for one last sea voyage, stocking my ship with many different goods. A storm hit our ship almost from the start. It blew us to the far ends of the earth to a place called the Land of Kings.

We had heard of this land and knew there were great sea serpents there. We had been told that when a ship passed by, a giant serpent would rise out of the ocean and swallow the ship whole.

We were telling stories of these terrible creatures when one of our crew spotted a serpent as big as a mountain coming out of the water toward us. Then we saw a second serpent and a third rising out of the water. Fearing for our lives, we fell to our knees and prayed to God, asking him to save us. A great storm rose, blowing our ship onto a great rock. The ship broke, and we were all sent into the sea.

I was able to swim to an island close by. After resting, I saw a stream that ran under a great mountain. I put together a small raft from some branches I found and traveled down the stream. Soon I heard the sound of rushing water. Before I knew it, I went over a great waterfall.

I was sure I would die, flying through the air and spray. But I did not. The good fishermen who live in that land cast out a net and saved me. An old man was among these fishermen, and he took me to his house.

I stayed there for many months. The people treated me well, giving me food and drink. Once a month, however, the people transformed in the strangest of ways. Their faces changed and they grew wings, turning into birds and flying far away.

One month, after the people had grown their wings and were preparing to fly off, I begged one of them to carry me with him. I flew so high that I could hear the angels singing.

Then there was great a lightning flash, and the creature dropped me on the top of a mountain. Two young men arrived. Telling me they were servants of God, they led me down the mountain. They told me that I had been in great danger, because the bird-men were servants of the devil. The two men led me to the shore, where a group of sailors were preparing for a sea voyage. I traveled with them and finally arrived back at home. My friends greeted me, and I was very happy to be home, swearing to God never to travel out to sea again.

"So now you know," said Sinbad the Sailor, "all the suffering I have gone through before enjoying the riches you see here."

"I beg you," replied the Sinbad the Porter, "forgive me for any wrong I have done in envying you."

After this, the porter never again complained of his station in life. He thought of how hard the merchant had worked for his riches, and all of the misery he himself had avoided. The two Sinbads lived on together in friendship until their time on earth had passed.

But morning drew near Scheherazade, and she fell silent. Dinarzad said to her sister, "Sister, what an amazing story!" Scheherazade replied, "It is nothing compared with what I will tell you tomorrow, if the king lets me live."

CHAPTER 8

The Tale of Aladdin

∽

THE THIRTY-FIRST NIGHT

The following night, when Scheherazade was in bed, her sister Dinarzad said, "Please, sister, tell us one of your lovely little tales." The king added, "Let it be more amazing than what came before." Scheherazade replied, "With the greatest pleasure!"

It is said, O great King, that there once was a poor tailor who lived in China with a son named Aladdin. The father worked very hard, while Aladdin was quite lazy and spent his days playing with other boys in the streets, returning home only for his daily meals.

The father kept working right up until the day he died. After this, Aladdin's mother sold the shop and started to spin yarn for cloth so the family could have money. Aladdin was fifteen years old then, and he continued in his lazy ways.

One day, a stranger came up to Aladdin. He told the boy he was his uncle and that he had come to pray at his dead brother's grave. The stranger returned home with Aladdin for dinner, and the man told his story, bringing Aladdin's mother to tears.

The next day, the stranger took Aladdin to the market and bought him new clothing. The uncle showed Aladdin the better parts of the city, and offered to put him to work as a merchant. Aladdin walked with the man for a long time. They left the city, passing the gardens beyond it and traveling up a high mountain.

Here the stranger built a fire. When it grew hot, he said a spell over it. The sky grew dark and the earth shook, opening up to reveal a great slab of marble. Aladdin was afraid, but the stranger told him to lift the slab and go down into the earth below.

"You will see three rooms, with jars full of silver and gold," he said. "But do not stop there. In the fourth room, there is a garden of fruit trees and a staircase leading up to an altar. Above this altar, you will find a lamp. Pour out the oil and bring the lamp back to me."

The stranger gave Aladdin a ring to wear for protection, and the boy went down into the earth. He did everything the stranger had told him to, but when he returned, he could not quite reach the top of the opening without help.

"O my son," the stranger told him, "give me the lamp so that I can help you climb up."

Aladdin was afraid to give the stranger the lamp and said, "No, Uncle, the lamp is safe with me. Give me your hand and help lift me out of this place."

The man asked again for the lamp, and Aladdin said no again. This went on for some time, and the stranger became more and more angry. Finally, the stranger closed the slab and said another spell, covering the slab with earth and leaving Aladdin trapped in the dark.

But morning drew near Scheherazade, and she fell silent. Dinarzad said to her sister, "Sister, what an amazing story!" Scheherazade replied, "It is nothing compared with what I will tell you tomorrow, if the king lets me live."

THE THIRTY-SECOND NIGHT

The following night, when Scheherazade was in bed, her sister Dinarzad said, "Please, sister, tell us more of this amazing tale." The king added, "Tell us more of what happened to Aladdin." Scheherazade replied, "With great pleasure!"

It is said, O great King, that the stranger was really a great wizard and that he had learned his art in Africa. There he had heard of a great treasure in China that lay buried in the earth. It was said that among the riches was a lamp that could make its owner more powerful than a thousand kings. The wizard had heard that only a certain poor boy of that city could remove the lamp from its resting place, and that the boy's name was Aladdin. So the wizard had come looking for the boy. He planned to use him to get the lamp and, afterward, to kill him.

Now Aladdin was trapped beneath the earth. He found that all the rooms had been closed. He cried and rubbed his hands together, calling upon God to deliver him. He happened to rub the ring the stranger had given him and, when he did so, a genie suddenly appeared before him. The genie said, "Ask what you wish, for I must obey whoever wears that ring on his finger."

Aladdin was overjoyed and asked the genie to put him back aboveground. Immediately the earth opened, and the boy was saved. Aladdin returned home and his mother wept with happiness, for she had not seen him for three days. Aladdin told her of everything that had happened to him. Then he went to sleep.

Aladdin slept for three days. When he woke up, his mother asked him to take some of the fabric she had woven to the market and sell it for food. The boy suggested selling the lamp instead, and his mother thought that was a good idea. She took a cloth and started to polish the lamp so that it looked nice for the sale. But suddenly a genie appeared before her. He was easily twice as powerful as the one Aladdin had seen before.

"Here I am," the genie said, in a voice that shook the earth they stood on. "I must obey whoever holds this lamp in their hands."

The mother fainted when the genie spoke, but Aladdin picked up the lamp and asked the genie for food. At this, the genie disappeared, returning moments later with three silver trays full of rich meats and bread that was whiter than snow.

Aladdin's mother was very scared. She told Aladdin to throw the lamp and the ring away. But the boy refused, and managed to calm her down. After they had eaten as much food as they could, Aladdin took one of the silver platters to the market and sold it for a lot of money.

In this way, Aladdin and his mother were never in need of money or food. Every few days, Aladdin would have the demon conjure more platters, and he would take them to sell. He was on his way to the market one day when he heard the loud sound of trumpets ring out. The king's daughter was near, and the street was being cleared so that she could pass by.

Aladdin hid behind a door as she passed by. He only saw the girl for a few seconds, but he instantly fell in love.

But morning drew near Scheherazade, and she fell silent. Dinarzad said to her sister, "Sister, what an amazing story!" Scheherazade replied, "It is nothing compared with what I will tell you tomorrow, if the king lets me live."

THE THIRTY-THIRD NIGHT

The following night, when Scheherazade was in bed, her sister Dinarzad said, "Please, sister, tell us more of this lovely tale." The king added, "Let it be the rest of Aladdin's tale." Scheherazade replied, "Certainly!"

It is said, O King, that Aladdin was full of love for the king's daughter. He returned home and begged his mother to ask the king if Aladdin could marry his daughter.

Aladdin's mother thought her son was mad, but Aladdin insisted. He rubbed the lamp to summon the genie and had him produce a gold bowl full of jewels. Aladdin then told his mother to bring these to the king as a gift.

With the jewels in a silk bag, Aladdin's mother went to the gates of the king's palace. She was kept there for a week before the king noticed her and asked his vizier to bring her before him.

The old woman told the king about her son's love for his daughter and his wish to marry her. The king laughed loudly at this and asked the old woman what she had brought him.

When he saw what she held, however, the king was very much amazed. The bright and heavy gems dazzled him, and he said, "I swear there is no one more worthy of my daughter than he who has given these jewels."

The king promised Aladdin's mother that his daughter would marry her son in three months. When those three months were up, Aladdin arrived at the palace at the head of a grand parade, with tall soldiers on black horses and beautiful girls carrying dishes of pure gold heaped with jewels.

The king welcomed the boy and seated him at his right side. There were long tables piled high with food. Everyone ate merrily. The wedding ceremony was performed, and the king's daughter became Aladdin's wife.

Back in Africa, the wizard heard of Aladdin's escape and the amazing things he had done. He returned to China and saw the palace Aladdin had built for his bride, with beautiful tiled walls and carpets woven with gold. The wizard knew that all this good fortune was because of the lamp. He swore that he would find it.

The wizard went to the market and had some lamps made. He took them and went through the streets of the town, crying, "Lamps! Lamps! Who will trade me an old lamp for one of these new ones?"

The people of the town thought the man was crazy, and many rushed to trade one of their old lamps for one of his new ones. The wizard made sure to pass by Aladdin's palace and call out loudly, "Lamps! Lamps! Who will trade me an old lamp for one of these new ones?"

One of the servants in the palace heard him and remembered seeing an old lamp that Aladdin kept on a shelf in his bedroom. She went to get it and traded it with the stranger, thinking to herself how wise she was and how foolish the old man was.

When the wizard saw that he had the lamp, he was delighted. He ran from the city and out into the desert beyond, making sure that no one had followed him. Then he rubbed the lamp. The great genie appeared, saying, "Here I am. I must obey whoever holds the lamp in his hands."

The wizard was very happy, and he told the genie to take the palace away from Aladdin and set it down in Africa.

"Shut your eyes," roared the genie's voice, "and you will find it all just as you say."

But morning drew near Scheherazade, and she fell silent. Dinarzad said to her sister, "Sister, what an amazing story!" Scheherazade replied, "It is nothing compared with what I will tell you tomorrow, if the king lets me live."

THE THIRTY-FOURTH NIGHT

The following night, when Scheherazade was in bed, her sister Dinarzad said, "Please, sister, tell us more of this lovely tale." The king added, "Let it be the end of the story of Aladdin." Scheherazade replied, "With great pleasure!"

It is told, O great King, that everything was done just as the wizard asked. In the morning, when the king looked out his window, he saw that

Aladdin's palace was gone, and he found that his daughter had disappeared also.

The king was angry and demanded that Aladdin be brought before him. The boy was put into chains, and the king ordered him to be locked up.

The people were quite sad at this. Aladdin fell to his knees and begged for the king's mercy. He said, "O great King, give me forty days to bring your daughter back and make it all as it was before. If forty days pass and I cannot do this, then lock me up and do what you will with me."

The king agreed, and Aladdin set out. He searched the city, then the desert, but found no trace of his palace or his wife. Aladdin was miserable. He threw himself to the ground, praying for God to help him.

While he prayed, Aladdin happened to rub one of his fingers against the wizard's ring. The genie appeared again before him.

"O genie," said Aladdin when he saw what had happened. "Bring me back my wife and my palace."

The genie replied, "That I cannot do. It is the work of the genie of the lamp. His power is stronger than mine."

Aladdin thought awhile and said, "Then put me down beside my palace."

The genie replied, "It will be done."

Aladdin closed his eyes. When he opened them, he was in Africa, outside his very own palace. He said his prayers, thanking God for saving him from his misery.

Aladdin went to his wife's room and stood outside her window, hoping she would see him. One of her servants was there, and she led him into the palace through a secret door. The princess was happy to see her husband. They hugged each other and cried with joy.

The princess told Aladdin how the wizard had taken the lamp and moved the palace, with all its people and riches. She told him that the wizard tried to win her love, offering jewels and gold. Aladdin listened to all that she said and thought carefully until he had come up with a plan. Then he kissed his wife and told her what he would do.

Aladdin sneaked carefully out of the palace and traveled toward the town. He met an old woman and paid her to trade her clothes for his. In this costume, Aladdin went to a shop in town and bought a powerful poison. Then he returned to the palace.

The wizard arrived, hoping to convince the princess to love him. That one time, she did not turn him away. Instead, she smiled at him, inviting him to dine with her. He sat with the princess while her servants laid the food on the table, so happy that he ate and drank without noticing that the princess did not take anything. Aladdin had secretly filled the wizard's cup with the poison. Instantly, he fell over.

Aladdin came out from the spot where he had been hiding. He searched the wizard and found the lamp hidden in his sleeve. He rubbed the lamp until the genie appeared, then he asked that the palace be returned to its original home.

The king was delighted when he saw that his daughter was safe and welcomed Aladdin back with open arms.

They all lived long and happily after that day. And when the king died, Aladdin took his place. The people were happy, for they loved him greatly, and Aladdin lived happily with the princess until the end of their days on earth.

But morning drew near Scheherazade, and she fell silent. Dinarzad said to her sister, "Sister, what an amazing story!" Scheherazade replied, "It is nothing compared with what I will tell you tomorrow, if the king lets me live."

CHAPTER 9

The Tale of Ali Baba and the Forty Thieves

⌒

THE THIRTY-FIFTH NIGHT

The following night, when Scheherazade was in bed, her sister Dinarzad said, "Please, sister, tell us one of your lovely little tales." The king added, "Let it be the most amazing tale yet." Scheherazade replied, "As you wish!"

It is said, O King, that there once lived in a town of Persia two brothers, Kasim and Ali Baba. When their father died, Kasim Baba married the daughter of a rich merchant, and when the merchant died, Kasim inherited his money. Ali married a woman named Morgiana, who was very poor but very clever, and he had to earn his living by gathering wood in the forest.

One day, while he was loading his wood to take to town, Ali Baba heard the sound of hooves and looked up to see forty horsemen approaching. The sight of the men scared Ali Baba, and he quickly hid in the bushes. As the men came nearer, Ali Baba saw that their horses were loaded with riches. They rode up to the face of a great rock, and the leader of the men cried, "Open sesame!"

Suddenly a wide door appeared in the rock, opening into a cave. The forty thieves rode in, and the door closed behind them. Ali Baba was amazed by what he had seen. Soon the door opened again and the men left, riding back the way they had come.

When Ali Baba was sure the men had gone, he approached the rock and repeated the words "Open sesame!"

The doorway appeared, and Ali Baba went inside. He found himself in a great room full of beautiful carpets, rolls of silk, and piles of gold and jewels. Ali Baba packed up as many gold coins as he could carry and rode home to his wife.

Ali Baba borrowed a scale from his brother so he could weigh the gold. His sister-in-law was curious to see what Ali Baba wanted to measure, so she coated the scale with wax. When the scale was returned, she found a gold coin stuck to it. She told her husband that Ali Baba was now rich and showed him the gold coin.

Kasim Baba went to talk to his brother, and Ali Baba told him everything that had happened at the great rock. Then Kasim Baba went to the cave alone and repeated, "Open sesame!"

The wide doorway opened, just as Ali Baba had said, and Kasim Baba went in, amazed at all the riches he saw before him. He spent a lot of time there, gathering so much treasure that he could barely move under the weight of it. The doorway had closed behind him, and Kasim Baba called out the words "Open barley!"

The doorway stayed closed. Kasim Baba had forgotten the spell. He called out many more things, but the door did not move. Kasim Baba was trapped inside. The next day, the forty thieves returned and found Kasim Baba still there. They quickly did away with him.

Ali Baba suspected what had happened. He gave his brother a burial and returned to the cave to take a few more bags of gold.

The forty thieves began to notice that some of their gold was missing. Their leader went to the town to see whether any man had died there recently and, if so, who. Once the thieves knew this, they might discover who had been working with the dead man.

The thieves' leader soon learned about Kasim, then found his way to Ali Baba's door. He marked the door with white chalk and returned to the cave to report all he learned.

Ali Baba's wife saw the chalk mark on the door and suspected danger. She took a piece of white chalk and marked all the other doors in the town. That night, the forty thieves rode into town, intending to kill Ali Baba, but when they saw that all the doors had been marked with white chalk they became greatly confused.

The next day, the leader returned and again found his way to Ali Baba's door. Being careful to remember it this time, he went back to the cave, and the thieves prepared forty large jars to hide in. They filled one jar with mustard seeds and hid thirty-nine of the thieves in the others. The leader loaded these jars onto mules and rode into town, pretending to be an oil merchant. He came to Ali Baba's house and knocked on the door, begging to be let in and given a room for the night.

Ali Baba took the man in and stored the jars with his animals behind the house. They were eating dinner when Morgiana went out behind the house to get a bit of oil.

As she got near the jars, she heard a voice ask, "Is it time?"

Morgiana quickly realized what had happened. She answered in a harsh voice, "The time is not yet come."

Then she hurried from jar to jar, repeating her message and sealing the jars so that the men could not escape. Morgiana then returned to the kitchen and poured some poison into a glass of wine. She served it to the leader of the thieves and he drank it up. Instantly, he fell over.

Ali Baba was angry at his wife, but then she pulled back the leader's cloak, showing Ali Baba the dagger he had hidden there to kill him with. She told him also of the thirty-nine thieves trapped in the jars outside.

Ali Baba covered her with kisses then and praised God for giving him such a wise wife. They lived happily after this, taking secretly from the great wealth still hidden in the cave.

Epilogue

Scheherazade entertained the king for many nights with these tales and, in the course of their life together, bore him three children. It is said that the king learned to love her, and she came to forgive him. The king had come to his senses, and he made amends by sparing her life and making her his queen. He cherished his wife and the stories she had told him, and they lived together in great happiness.

What Do *You* Think?
Questions for Discussion

∽

Have you ever been around a toddler who keeps asking the question "Why?" Does your teacher call on you in class with questions from your homework? Do your parents ask you questions about your day at the dinner table? We are always surrounded by questions that need a specific response. But is it possible to have a question with no right answer?

The following questions are about the book you just read. But this is not a quiz! They are designed to help you look at the people, places, and events in the story from different angles. These questions do not have specific answers. Instead, they might make you think of the story in a completely new way.

Think carefully about each question and enjoy discovering more about this classic story.

1. Why does Scheherazade tell the king a new story every night? Who tells you stories?

2. In "The Tale of the Merchant and His Wife," the old man tells the merchant "your promise to return here is a brave one." Do you agree? What is the bravest thing you have ever done?

3. In "The Tale of the Merchant and His Wife," the old man tells the demon that his story is even more amazing than the merchant's story. Do you agree? What is the strangest thing that has ever happened to you?

4. How does the fisherman convince the genie to help him? Can you think of any other

way that the fisherman might have outsmarted the genie?

5. In "The Porter's Tale," the sign above the door reads, "For those who meddle in the concerns of others, the punishment will be great." What do you think this means? Have you ever tried to learn about something that was none of your business?

6. How is "The Porter's Tale" similar to the book's main story? Which dervishes' story was your favorite? Which of Scheherazade's tales did you most enjoy?

7. Sinbad the Sailor has a great number of misadventures. Why do you suppose he continues to travel? Where would you most like to travel to?

8. When Aladdin goes below ground he finds a magical lamp with a wish-granting genie inside. What would you wish for if you found such a lamp?

9. How does the wizard get Aladdin's lamp? Has anyone ever taken something of yours without your permission?

10. Ali Baba's wife is said to be very clever. Do you agree? How does she save her husband from the thieves? What is the cleverest thing you've ever done?

Afterword

by Arthur Pober, EdD

❧

First impressions are important.

Whether we are meeting new people, going to new places, or picking up a book unknown to us, first impressions count for a lot. They can lead to warm, lasting memories or can make us shy away from any future encounters.

Can you recall your own first impressions and earliest memories of reading the classics?

Do you remember wading through pages and pages of text to prepare for an exam? Or were you the child who hid under the blanket to read with a flashlight, joining forces with Robin Hood to save Maid Marian? Do you only remember how long it took you to read a lengthy novel such as *Little Women*? Or did you become best friends with the March sisters?

Even for a gifted young reader, getting through long chapters with dense language can easily become overwhelming and can obscure the richness of the story and its characters. Reading an abridged, newly crafted version of a classic novel can be the gentle introduction a child needs to explore the characters and storyline without the frustration of difficult vocabulary and complex themes.

Reading an abridged version of a classic novel gives the young reader a sense of independence and the satisfaction of finishing a "grown-up" book. And when a child is engaged with and inspired by a classic story, the tone is set for further exploration of the story's themes, characters, history, and details. As a child's reading skills advance, the desire to tackle the original, unabridged version of the story will naturally emerge.

If made accessible to young readers, these stories can become invaluable tools for understanding themselves in the context of their families and social environments. This is why the Classic Starts series includes questions that stimulate discussion regarding the impact and social relevance of the characters and stories today. These questions can foster lively conversations between children and their parents or teachers. When we look at the issues, values, and standards of past times in terms of how we live now, we can appreciate literature's classic tales in a very personal and engaging way.

Share your love of reading the classics with a young child, and introduce an imaginary world real enough to last a lifetime.

Dr. Arthur Pober, EdD

Dr. Arthur Pober has spent more than twenty years in the fields of early childhood and gifted education. He is the former principal of one of the world's oldest laboratory schools for gifted youngsters, Hunter College Elementary School, and former Director of Magnet Schools for the Gifted and Talented for more than 25,000 youngsters in New York City.

Dr. Pober is a recognized authority in the areas of media and child protection and is currently the U.S. representative to the European Institute for the Media and European Advertising Standards Alliance.

Explore these wonderful stories in our
Classic Starts™ library.